ISABELLA'S GARDEN

GLENDA MILLARD
illustrated by REBECCA COOL

CANDLEWICK PRESS

This is the soil,
all dark and deep,
in Isabella's garden.

These are the seeds
that sleep in the soil,
all dark and deep, in Isabella's garden.

This is the rain that soaks the seeds
that sleep in the soil,
all dark and deep, in Isabella's garden.

These are the clouds that cry the rain
that soaks the seeds that sleep in the soil,
all dark and deep, in Isabella's garden.

This is the sun that kisses the clouds
that cried the rain that soaked the seeds
that slept in the soil, all dark and deep,
in Isabella's garden.

These are the shoots that seek the sun
that kissed the clouds that cried the rain
that soaked the seeds that slept in the soil,
all dark and deep, in Isabella's garden.

These are the flowers that waltz with the wind
that ruffles the buds, all velvety skinned,
that swelled the shoots that sought the sun

that kissed the clouds that cried the rain
that soaked the seeds that slept in the soil,
all dark and deep, in Isabella's garden.

This is the chick
in the thistledown vest
that was hatched by the bird
with the scarlet breast
that sang while the buttercups
waltzed with the wind

that ruffled the buds, all velvety skinned,
that swelled the shoots that sought the sun
that kissed the clouds that cried the rain
that soaked the seeds that slept in the soil,
all dark and deep, in Isabella's garden.

This is the climbing tree, leafy and appled,

that speckles the garden with shade, deep and dappled,

that shelters the chick in the thistledown vest

that was hatched by the bird with the scarlet breast

that sang while the buttercups waltzed with the wind

that ruffled the buds, all velvety skinned,

that swelled the shoots that sought the sun

that kissed the clouds that cried the rain

that soaked the seeds that slept in the soil,

all dark and deep, in Isabella's garden.

These are the leaves, turning crimson and gold,

that brighten the branches as evenings grow cold

that cling to the tree that was once green and appled

that speckled the garden with shade, deep and dappled,

that sheltered the fledgling, in feathers now dressed,

that was hatched by the bird with the scarlet breast

that sang while the buttercups waltzed with the wind

that ruffled the buds, all velvety skinned,

that swelled the shoots that sought the sun

that kissed the clouds that cried the rain

that soaked the seeds that slept in the soil,

all dark and deep, in Isabella's garden.

This is the mantis that prays to the moon
that winter come never or not quite so soon
and sighs at the leaves,
now crimson and gold,
that tremble and tumble
on evenings grown cold

and lie 'neath the tree that was once green and appled
that speckled the garden with shade, deep and dappled,
that sheltered the fledgling, now flown from his nest,

that was missed by the bird

with the scarlet breast

that wept when the petals were tossed by the wind

that ruffled the buds, all velvety skinned,

that swelled the shoots that sought the sun

that kissed the clouds that cried the rain

that soaked the seeds that slept in the soil,

all dark and deep, in Isabella's garden.

But despite what the mantis begged of the moon,
winter comes swiftly and silent and soon.

Jack Frost spreads his mantle of sequins and shimmer,
encrusting the garden with glisten and glimmer.

Till all that remains is the well-feathered nest
that was built by the bird with the scarlet breast
and a handful of seeds for the wild wind to blow.
Enough, just enough, for a garden to grow.

These are the seeds
that sleep in the soil,
all dark and deep,
in Isabella's garden.

For Hannah Isabell Millard.
Seasons come and seasons go, but the gardens you have planted
will live forever in our hearts.
G. M.

For Ross
R. C.

First U.S. edition 2012

Library of Congress Cataloging-in-Publication Data is available.

Library of Congress Catalog Card Number pending

ISBN 978-0-7636-6016-1

11 12 13 14 15 16 SCP 10 9 8 7 6 5 4 3 2 1

Printed in Humen, Dongguan, China

This book was typeset in Caslon Antique.
The illustrations were done in mixed media.

Candlewick Press
99 Dover Street
Somerville, Massachusetts 02144

visit us at www.candlewick.com